Little Quack's New Friend

by Lauren Thompson   pictures by Derek Anderson

Simon & Schuster Books for Young Readers

NEW YORK LONDON TORONTO SYDNEY

Mama Duck had five little ducklings, Widdle, Waddle, Piddle, Puddle, and Little Quack.
They all played together in the cool, shady pond.

One day, out jumped a teeny green frog.
"Ribbit, ribbit! I'm Little Ribbit!" he said. "Can I play?"

"No way," said Widdle. "You're too tiny!"
"And you're too green!" said Waddle.
"And you can't quack!" said Piddle.
"And you're a FROG!" said Puddle.
"That's okay!" said Little Quack. "*I* want to play!"

So—*quack, quack, ribbit, ribbit!*—
two little friends went off to play.

Over by the reeds Little Ribbit said, "Let's splash!"
"I love to splash!" said Little Quack.
Splishy, splosh!
"Can I splash with you?" asked Widdle.

"Sure!" said Little Ribbit.
Splishy, sploshy, splish! splashed three wet friends.

Over in the mud Little Ribbit said, "Let's squish!"
"We love to squish!" said Widdle and Little Quack.
Squashy, squooshy, squash!
"Can I squish with you?" asked Waddle.

"Of course!" said Little Ribbit.
Squashy, squooshy, squashy, squoosh!
squished four muddy friends.

Up on the log Little Ribbit said, "Let's bounce!"
"We love to bounce!" said Widdle, Waddle, and
Little Quack.
Boingo, poingo, boingo, poing!
"Can I bounce with you?" asked Piddle.

"Why not?" said Little Ribbit.
Boingo, poingo, boingo, poingo, boing!
bounced five hoppy friends.

Down by the lily pads Little Ribbit said,
"Let's dunk!"
"We love to dunk!" said Widdle, Waddle,
Piddle, and Little Quack.
Plunka, splunka, plunka, splunka, plunk!
"Can I dunk with you?" asked Puddle.

"Come on over!" said Little Ribbit.
Plunka, splunka, plunka, splunka, plunka, splunk!
dunked six bottoms-up friends.

Then Widdle said to Little Ribbit, "You know what?
It's okay if you're tiny!"
"And it's okay if you're green!" said Waddle.
"And it's okay if you can't quack!" said Piddle.
"And it's okay if you're a FROG!" said Puddle.
"We *all* like to play!" said Little Quack.

Then—*splishy, sploshy, squashy, squooshy, poingo, boingo, plunka, splunka!*—how they played!

"Hooray for Little Ribbit,
our *ribbitty* new friend!"

To Owen, our *plunka,*
splunka duckling!
—L. T.

For Ethan, Jonah,
Justin, and Kaden
—D. A.

SIMON & SCHUSTER BOOKS FOR YOUNG READERS
An imprint of Simon & Schuster Children's Publishing Division
1230 Avenue of the Americas, New York, New York 10020

SIMON & SCHUSTER BOOKS FOR YOUNG READERS is a trademark of Simon & Schuster, Inc.
Book design by Greg Stadnyk
The text for this book is set in Stone Informal and 99.
The illustrations for this book are rendered in acrylic on Arches hot press watercolor paper.
Manufactured in China
2 4 6 8 10 9 7 5 3 1
Library of Congress Cataloging-in-Publication Data
Thompson, Lauren.
Little Quack's new friend / Lauren Thompson ; illustrated by Derek Anderson.— 1st ed.
p. cm.
Summary: When a frog invites five ducklings to play, four refuse because he is too little and
green, but Little Quack has so much fun with his new friend that the other ducklings soon join in.
ISBN-13: 978-0-689-86893-1
ISBN-10:   0-689-86893-6
[1. Ducks—Fiction. 2. Frogs—Fiction. 3. Play—Fiction. 4. Friendship—Fiction. 5. Ponds—Fiction.]
I. Anderson, Derek, 1969- ill. II. Title. PZ7.T37163Lkn 2006 [E]—dc22

first
edition